A FRIEND IN THE LIBRARY

FICTION

BY

EVA MARCH TAPPAN

British Library Cataloguing-in-Publication Data
A catalogue record for this book is available from the
British Library

FICTION

A FRIEND IN THE LIBRARY

A Practical Guide to the Writings of

RALPH WALDO EMERSON

NATHANIEL HAWTHORNE

HENRY WADSWORTH LONGFELLOW

JAMES RUSSELL LOWELL

JOHN GREENLEAF WHITTIER

OLIVER WENDELL HOLMES

IN TWELVE VOLUMES

VOLUME X

FICTION

EVERYBODY likes stories of one sort or another. It is a delightful rest and change to close the door on all troublesome questions and step into a new world wherein all things move on smoothly, or where, if anything does go wrong, you know it is only a part of the plot, and will be straightened out in a little while.

The "short story" is a special favorite at present. It differs from the novel in other qualities than length. In the long story there is usually a series of incidents that develop a plot; in the short story, the interest centres in the situation. In Hawthorne's "Rappaccini's Daughter" (iv. 125), with its playful introduction, there is no chain of incidents, but

there is a remarkable situation. A wonder-
fully beautiful girl has always been nourished
on poisons until her breath and touch have
become fatal to whatever approaches her.
She is loved by the young Giovanni, who
knows nothing of this terrible fact. What will
be the result? Will the maiden die? Will she
be cured by the coming of love into her life?
Will Giovanni flee from her in horror? Will
his love for her hold him fast in her bonds for
life or for death? Will he, too, become as
poisonous a thing as herself? Will she, how-
ever unwillingly, exercise her murderous
power upon the man whom she loves? This
is the situation, and the writer must show his
skill in his treatment of it.

In "Peter Goldthwaite's Treasure" (ii.
204), another of Hawthorne's short stories,

the old man Peter, "so gaunt and threadbare that . . . the scarecrows in the cornfields beckoned to him, as he passed by," is convinced that somewhere in his cottage one of his ancestors has hidden away a chest of treasure. Hoping to find it, he begins to tear the house down; and as he lays about him with his axe, old Tabitha burns up beams and mouldings and panels, "for she wisely considered that, without a house, they should need no wood to warm it; and therefore economy was nonsense." This is the situation, an old man searching for visionary wealth and refusing a substantial offer for the lot whereon his cottage stands. How will the story end? Will Peter find no treasure? Will the house tumble about his ears? Will he die before the search is completed? Will he really discover a chest of gold? There is a problem to be solved; what will the answer be? In Hawthorne's solution, the chest is found, the rusty key is turned in the rusty lock; and here are "bills of credit, treasury notes, and bills of land," but —

It is not easy to write a good short story. The situation must be made clear, not by leisurely pages of description, but by hints and bits of conversation. The situation must be somewhat unusual, or it will not catch the attention of the reader. The problem must not be too simple, for there must be several possible ways of solving it. And, finally, there must be a solution that is not commonplace. To accomplish all this within the limits of a story that may be read in half an hour demands a strict economy of words. Every phrase must be worth while. Every detail must lead on to the close. Every thought must have a connection with the ending of the story.

The writer of a novel has in one respect a much more simple task; he has room enough. His descriptions may be more full and complete. His conversations need not be so strictly limited to bringing out the special points that are called for. On the other hand, he must have the imagination to introduce plausible incidents; he must not only present a problem to be solved, but he must keep up interest in the problem for several hundred pages; and his solution must, of course, be as original and as satisfactory as would be required in a short story.

In Holmes's "Elsie Venner" (v.) a somewhat startling problem is laid before us. Before Elsie's birth her mother is bitten by a rattlesnake. When Elsie appears in the story, she is a young girl of wild, dazzling beauty; but she walks "with a peculiar undulation of movement"; she wears a dress "of a curious pattern, and a camel's-hair scarf twisted a little fantastically about her." Around her neck there is always a chain or necklace of some sort, and this she twists and coils and braids. A serpent bracelet with emerald eyes is one of her favorite ornaments. She speaks with a "sibilant utterance"; her eyes have a strange, cold glitter, and when she is angry, they narrow and her forehead seems to draw down and flatten. When the fancy strikes her, at any hour of day or night, she wanders off on the mountain to a ledge that is the home of scores of rattlesnakes. When she is weary, she often throws herself down "in a careless coil" upon a tiger's-skin in one corner of her room. With all her beauty, she is so uncanny that her sensitive teacher slips away and washes the tips of her fingers after she has been obliged to touch those of the girl.

Such is the central character of the book. Elsie's father is a man of wealth. He yields to every whim of the daughter, who is to him both repulsive and beloved, hoping that some time the human nature will overcome the reptilian. Around the girl moves on the usual life of an old New England village. Occasionally she takes some small part in it; but wherever she goes, there is always a distance between her and others.

Holmes says in his preface (ix.) that the

real aim of the story is "to test the doctrine of 'original sin' and human responsibility for the disordered volition coming under that technical denomination." The tale may easily set one to thinking on questions of moral responsibility, but the name which Holmes gives to it further on, "a physiological romance," describes it most excellently. When we read the book, we are less interested in the question whether Elsie is to be blamed for what would be evil in a normal human being than in whether the serpent nature or the woman nature will triumph. Will she become more and more a thing of horror? Will she commit some crime that will bring upon her the penalties inflicted upon an ordinary criminal? Will her attraction to the young man who has become her teacher grow into a love so strong as to humanize her? Will the mark about her throat, the visible sign of her humiliation, ever disappear? This is the problem for the author to solve. He has solved it most artistically. There is one ending which is inevitable. He has found it, and has presented it in a few lines wherein every word is glowing with significance.

This book is far more than the "medicated novel" which one of Dr. Holmes's friends called it; for, like every other book that has come from his pen, it gleams with thoughts and suggestions that set our own thoughts to work; for instance, his word of sympathy for "everybody that sighs for earthly remembrance in a planet with a core of fire and a crust of fossils!" He often tosses problems before us. Here is one: —

A man is stunned by a blow with a stick on the head. He becomes unconscious. Another man gets a harder blow on the head from a bigger stick, and it kills him. Does he become unconscious, too? If so, *when does he come to his consciousness?* The man who has a slight or moderate blow comes to himself when the immediate shock passes off and the organs begin to work again, or when a bit of the skull is pried up, if that happens to be broken. Suppose the blow is hard enough to spoil the brain and stop the play of the organs, what happens then?

Holmes's "The Guardian Angel" (vi.) is especially full of these stray bits of questioning thought. The old doctor who has known the family of the heroine for five generations says:—

It seems to me that I can see something of almost every one of 'em in this child's face,—it's the forehead of this one, and it's the eyes of that one, and it's that other's mouth, and the look that I remember in another, and when she speaks, why, I've heard that same voice before.

Elsewhere he says:—

The lives of our progenitors are, as we know, reproduced in ourselves. *Whether they as individuals have any consciousness of it*, is another matter. It is possible that they do get a second as it were fractional life in us.

It is upon this idea of inherited traits that the story of "The Guardian Angel" is founded. Little Myrtle Hazard is the heroine. Among her ancestors was one Ann Holyoake, who was burned as a martyr. The story had come down that, after the fagots were kindled, she had said in a prayer, "Thou hast made a covenant, O Lord, with me and my children forever"; and the legend was still half believed that she acted as guardian angel to each of her descendants.

Even if one does not care about considering questions of "fractional lives," there is plenty of interest in the story itself. Myrtle has a bit of Indian blood in her veins. She was born in the tropics, left an orphan, brought to New England as a baby, and delivered into the hands of Miss Silence Withers — a suggestive name. Miss Silence determines to do her conscientious best for the child, but she knows "no more about children and their ways and wants than if she had been a female ostrich." Myrtle must "have her will broken," Miss Silence believes; but small Myrtle refuses, even at the age of four, to yield to the most heroic treatment. Before she has come to her fifteenth year, she has shown herself a girl whom neither "catechising, nor advising, nor punishing" ever affected, and now there follows an escapade, wild but not wicked. She is saved even from gossip by her old teacher and friend, Byles Gridley. Then comes the struggle between her natures, the nature of the martyr, of the Indian, and of a beautiful ancestress whose bracelet she wears. The old schoolmaster is charity itself. He watches over Myrtle, and he has sympathy for even one Gifted Hopkins, who fancies himself a poet. There is a large estate in the clutches of the law; there is a villain, a legal paper with blotches of ink on the back of it, there is a faithful servant and a scheming visitor, there is an honorable man of talent who finds himself bound to a simple little girl now entirely out of his sphere — and does not know that the simple little girl is appreciating the rhymes of Gifted Hopkins far more than his own talents. There are the foundling twins to whom Master Gridley gave in an hour of merriment the names of Isosceles and Helminthia. There are all these characters and others almost as interesting; but what they do and say and think, what the fate of the heroine is, whether the martyred ancestor, or the lady of the bracelet, or who, proves to be the guardian angel, must be left to the author to reveal.

The cheery little heroine of "The House of the Seven Gables" (Hawthorne, vii.) has no birth-taint, and hardly a trace of ancestral peculiarities. The House "lets in the wind and rain, and the snow, too, in the garret and upper chambers, in winter-time, but it never

lets in the sunshine." Its mistress, poor old
Hepzibah, has little to live on save "the shad-
owy food of aristocratic reminiscences," and
in great agony of mind at breaking through
the traditions of her descent, she has opened a
little shop. Hepzibah has no commercial in-
stincts, and the struggles of her first day result
in nothing more than "half a dozen coppers
and a questionable ninepence," and a vague
memory of many blunders. Just at this time,
Phœbe, the healthy, sunny, light-hearted little
country cousin, steps out of the omnibus and
into the sombre life of the House as easily and
naturally as a bird flits from one tree to another. Hepzibah's life centres in the return of
her brother Clifford from a mysterious ab-
sence of many years, with which their wealthy
cousin Jaffrey Pyncheon has had something

to do. Driven by stern necessity, she has
rented a room to one Holgrave, who can take
daguerreotypes — and in the time of writing
this romance a daguerreotype was far more of
a wonder than are to-day all the marvels of
electricity. Phœbe and Holgrave, the only
young things about the House, find much in
common; and one may guess the ending of
the story in that respect. But justice must be
done to Hepzibah and Clifford, so far as "justice" can make up for undeserved sufferings.
Retribution must come to the guilty, and the
winning old optimist, Uncle Venner, must be
kept from ending his days at "my farm," as
he cheerfully calls the poorhouse. Hawthorne's wife was charmed with the "dear
home-loveliness and satisfaction" of the clos-
ing pages of the story, and their contrast with

the "sterner tragedy of the commencement";
and I cannot imagine that any subsequent
reader has ever failed to agree with her.

Holmes brings us face to face with strange
questionings and scientific possibilities; Hawthorne suggests weird fancies and half hu-
morous poetic conceits. The famous Pyncheon breed of hens, for instance, has dwin-
dled with the diminishing fortunes of the
family, and the fowls' distinguishing crest is
"oddly and wickedly analogous to Hepzibah's turban." Of the old harpsichord, which
has been closed for many years, he says, there
must be "a vast deal of dead music in it,
stifled for want of air." In Hawthorne's
"Scarlet Letter" (vi.) the story opens on a
bright, sunny morning. A throng of men "in
sad-colored garments and gray, steeple-

crowned hats, intermixed with women, some wearing hoods and others bare-headed," stand before the jail of colonial Boston. The door is flung open, and a handsome young woman, Hester Prynne, steps forth. A baby is in her arms. She walks slowly up the wooden steps leading to the pillory. On the breast of her gown is the letter A, which the magistrates have condemned her to wear throughout her life as the badge of her shame. The Reverend Arthur Dimmesdale is bidden to exhort her that she make full confession and name the father of her child. She refuses to speak. The husband whom she has wronged appears on the scene, a stranger to all in the place. For years he devotes his powers to the mental torture of the man whom he suspects. On the day of his death this man ascends feebly the stairs of the pillory and reveals to the people his sin and his suffering. This is all that the romance has of story; and yet one who opens the book can hardly lay it aside until he reaches *"on a field, sable, the letter* A, Gules,*"* which is its conclusion. The publisher Fields began to read the manuscript and read straight on through the night.

The wonder of this book is its fearful keenness of insight, its terrible accuracy in the delineation of one actor after another in the awful drama of sin. The old tales of magic seem almost to have come true when one sees how easily Hawthorne reads the hearts of these people whom he has created. With Hester, sin is brought to the light, it is seen of all, it is punished openly and severely. With that other, it is hidden, it is known only to himself. Hawthorne knows the hearts of both and lays their inmost feelings before us. Retribution of sin may take more than one form, but it is inevitable. Happy is the sinner to whom punishment and repentance have brought forth their proper fruit in the development and growth of character. Such is the teaching of "The Scarlet Letter," the greatest American novel. The atmosphere of the book is not so much gloom and darkness as intensity. One feels as if in the midst of irresistible unseen powers. Even the child, little Pearl, beautiful, fascinating, but so elfish and capricious that her mother almost questions whether she is a human child — even the child Pearl is as intense in her way as Hester herself. The sin of her parents is visited upon her in her innocence; but at the end of the book Hawthorne hints at the happiness that has come to her in some foreign land; and also at a warmth of love and interest which makes its way across the ocean to Hester's little cottage by the seashore.

A writer like Hawthorne, who could throw the glamour of romance over the sternest features of the early colonial days, could hardly help reveling in the mellowed literary and artistic atmosphere of Italy. The result of his stay in that country was "The Marble Faun" (ix., x.). In this romance four people are brought together. Two of them are painters, Hilda, the Puritan maiden who makes her Roman home in the top of a lofty tower around which the white doves circle and come at her call; and Miriam, who is handsome, generous, and fascinating. Miriam is adored by a young Italian, Donatello, who represents, as nearly as even Hawthorne might venture it, the faun of the days of mythology. Miriam's smile and an hour of sunshine are enough to make him radiant with happiness. The fourth member of the little comradeship is the sculptor Kenyon, practical, reasonable, and a good friend to whoever comes in his way. About Miriam's past life there is a mysterious silence. A repulsive stranger, equally mysterious, recognizes her in the catacombs, and pursues her relentlessly. These are the principal characters. The one event of the story is a sudden murder by one of the four. The tale is a profound study of the effect which this crime produces on the murderer and the other three, according to that " fatal decree by which every crime is made to be the agony of many innocent persons as well as of the single guilty one"; and it brings into relief the bold question whether sin "has been so beneficently handled by omniscience and omnipotence, that . . . it has really become an instrument most effective in the education of intellect and soul."

"The Marble Faun" is less intense than "The Scarlet Letter." The surroundings are not those of a Puritan village, but of Rome, the rich, the wonderful, and, even in its decay, the glorious. The book is full of descriptions of the Eternal City. Hawthorne himself says that he is surprised to see to what an extent he has introduced them. He would have made no claim to any profound knowledge of art; but his criticisms of various sculptures and paintings are so reasonable and sensible and appreciative that they are far beyond the chatter of many so-called critics. He says that Mr. Story's Cleopatra is marked by "a marvelous repose"; Guido's Archangel Michael should not wear "a dainty air of the first celestial society," but should look like one who has been through a severe struggle with the dragon under his foot; the Laocoön is like "the tumult of Niagara, which ceases to be tumult because it lasts forever"; Hilda searches the galleries in vain for a Virgin who shall wear "a face of celestial beauty, but human as well as heavenly, and with the shadow of past grief upon it; bright with immortal youth, yet matronly and motherly; and endowed with a queenly dignity, but infinitely tender, as the highest and deepest attribute of her divinity." The bronze statue of Marcus Aurelius is "the most majestic representation of the kingly character that ever the world has seen."

In Emerson's essay on "Books" (vii. 187), he says that for the most part the foundation of the novel is "She was beautiful and he fell in love." But the novels of the best writers are of quite a different caste. With Hawthorne in particular, although the story is always interesting, it is not of the first importance. If it were possible to strike out every trace of plot, they would still be literary masterpieces, so perfect is the author's "awful power of insight." He knows the "domesticated sunbeam," Phœbe, the struggling, unselfish Hepzibah, the false-hearted Judge Pyncheon, the tricksy, whimsical little Pearl, the faunlike Donatello, and the white-souled Hilda, equally well; and he can reveal them to us with the lightning flashes of genius.

But the world is full of novels. How is one to know what to choose? How can one who is not a literary expert decide whether the volume of fiction which has entertained him is good literature or is of no use but to amuse him for an hour of rest? There are a few simple tests, and any one who is willing to do a little thinking can tell for himself whether a novel is trash or treasure. In the first place, the plot may be slender or complicated, but, granting that the characters possess the traits ascribed to them by the author, it must be probable, and every page must count toward its development. The descriptions must be so vivid that, as you read, you can form a picture in your mind of the person or place described. The conversation must be natural and true to the persons speaking. The characters must be true to life, and they must grow. Elsie Venner, Hester, Donatello, Hilda, are far different at the end of the story from what they are at its beginning; and they have not been arbitrarily altered, they have developed, they manifest only that change and growth which the conditions of their lives would naturally bring about in such persons. Even in Hawthorne's romances, wherein the whole scene of action is raised to an atmosphere very different from that of our every-day life, even there each character must be true to himself, must act and speak as such a person would in such an atmosphere. Finally, no story is worth reading unless its moral is good, unless as you think back over the narrative you feel the teaching of the book to be in favor of what is pure and noble and generous and faithful. The fiction that meets these requirements is more than an idle amusement for an empty hour; it is truth itself.

FICTION

ADDITIONAL

HOLMES

A Mortal Antipathy, vii.

WHITTIER

Margaret Smith's Journal, ix.

LONGFELLOW

Kavanagh, viii.
Hyperion, viii.
Martin Franc, and also other stories in vol. vii.

HAWTHORNE

Mosses from an Old Manse, iv., v.
Twice-Told Tales, i., ii.
The Blithedale Romance, viii.
Dr. Grimshawe's Secret, xv.
The Dolliver Romance, xiv.
Ethan Brand; also other stories in vol. iii.
Fanshawe, xvi; of interest as being Hawthorne's first long story.

QUESTIONS

1. What is the distinguishing characteristic of the "short story"?

   Its interest centres in a situation rather than in a plot.

2. Name one of the greatest masters of the short story.

   Nathaniel Hawthorne.

3. Why is it especially difficult to write a good short story?

   Because everything must be so condensed.

4. In what respect is the writing of a novel a more simple task?

   The writer has room enough.

5. In what respect is it more difficult?

   The interest must be so long sustained.

6. What was the aim of Holmes's "Elsie Venner" (v.)?

   To test the doctrine of "original sin."

FICTION

7. How does Holmes describe the book?
   As "a physiological romance."

8. What special advantage is there in reading
   Holmes's novels?"
   They set our own minds to work.

9. What is the subject of "The Guardian
   Angel" (vi.)?
   *The reproduction of the lives of our ances-
   tors in ourselves.*

10. What does Hawthorne's wife say of the close
    of "The House of the Seven Gables"
    (vii.)?
    *She contrasts its " dear home-loveliness and
    satisfaction" with the " sterner tragedy
    of the commencement."*

11. How does Hawthorne set our imagination
    to work?
    By his weird fancies and poetic conceits.

12. What is the most marked characteristic of Hawthorne's romances?

   The "awful power of insight" displayed in them.

13. What is the literary rank of "The Scarlet Letter"?

   It is the greatest American novel.

14. What was the literary result of Hawthorne's stay in Italy?

   "The Marble Faun" (ix., x.).

15. What is the aim of the book?

   To portray the effect of a crime on different persons.

16. How does the atmosphere of this book differ from that of "The Scarlet Letter" (vi.)?

   It is far less intense.

17. Besides the delineations of character, how else is the book of value?

   In the charm of its style, its beautiful de-

scriptions of Rome, and its appreciative art criticisms.

18. Is the plot of the first importance in Hawthorne's books?

    No, if every trace of plot could be struck out, they would still be literary masterpieces.

19. Name some tests of a good novel.

    The plot must be probable to the characters, and every page must count in its development; the descriptions must be vivid, the conversation natural, the characters true to life, and they must grow; and the book must have a good moral.

20. How can Hawthorne's characters be "true to life" when we never meet people just like them?

    They are consistent with themselves. They act and speak as such persons would under such circumstances and conditions.